# DAVE'S HAIRCUT

by
Damon
Burnard

**Dutton Children's Books**

NEW YORK

For anyone who has ever had a *BAD* haircut

Copyright © 2003 by Damon Burnard
All rights reserved.

CIP Data is available.

Published in the United States 2003 by Dutton Children's Books,
a division of Penguin Putnam Books for Young Readers
345 Hudson Street, New York, New York 10014
www.penguinputnam.com

Designed by Tim Hall
Printed in China
ISBN 0-525-46967-2
First Edition
1 3 5 7 9 10 8 6 4 2

Nothing.

Nada.

*Zilch.*

**MOM!**

shouted Dave.

**Quick!**

**THE SUN'S GONE OUT!**

Dave's mom came in. . . .

"**NONSENSE!**" she said.

"Your hair is in your eyes, that's all!"

And she brushed it away.

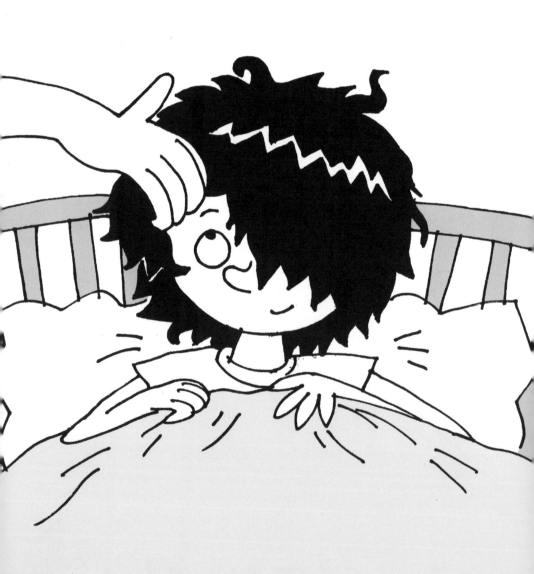

"What you need is a **HAiRcuT**," said Dave's mom.

**"HAiRcuT?"** said Dave.

# "You'll never take me ALIVE!"

yelled Dave.

Dave's last haircut was a .

Dave's dad had taken him to Frank's Barbershop.

Frank's fingers smelled of pickles and cigarettes, and he never took his eyes off the TV.

The next day at school was a

# NIGHTMARE.

Micky Badazz made fun of him . . .

. . . and everyone LAUGHED.

Zorro, the class bunny, hid from him . . .

. . . and Lunchlady Lily felt so sorry for
him, she gave him an extra scoop of
mashed potatoes.

And Rosie Sky—the girl Dave had secretly loved since the first grade?

Rosie didn't laugh. She kind of blushed and said "Hi!" as though nothing had happened, when in fact she and Dave knew something *TERRIBLE* had happened . . .

Dave had a **BAD** haircut.

# "NEVER AGAIN!"

yelled Dave.

"Come on, Dave!" said Dave's mom. "You can't stay under there forever!"

"We'll see about that!" said Dave.

But Dave's mom was smart, and she did a very smart thing. . . .

She put a bowl of Super-Choco Puff Pops in the middle of the bedroom floor.

"Super-Choco Puff Pops!" said Dave.
"My *favorite!*"

. . . . And out he came . . . .

"So how come you don't want a haircut?"
asked Dave's mom.

That seemed like a DUMB question to Dave.

He thought about ALL the BAD haircuts he could end up getting.

Like...

**AND THEN** Dave thought about how BIG his ears would look....

**AND THEN** Dave thought about Micky Badazz making *fun* of him....

"Why won't I get a haircut?"
said Dave.

And he did.

yelled Dave's mom.

"That's enough already! This time we'll go to Uncle Danny's barber."

"Do I have to?" asked Dave.

"Yes," said Dave's mom. "Don't worry. Uncle Danny's hair always looks *great!*"

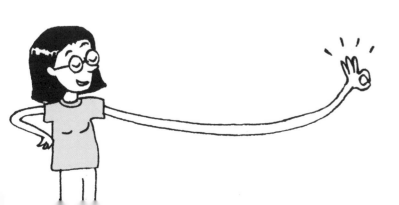

**"NO WAY!"** shouted Dave,
and he ran into the bathroom.

And then he had an idea.

Barbers are EVIL! thought Dave.
If I have to get a haircut,

And he did.

SNiP!
SNiP!

went Dave's
silver scissors. . . .

FLiP!
FLOP!

went his hair
on the floor. . . .

And

then

Dave

**LOOKED**

in

the

mirror.

Dave's mom peeked inside.

"Oh dear," she said.
"Oh deary, deary me."

Dave put a paper
bag on his head
to hide his haircut . . .

. . . then off they went to Uncle Danny's barber.

At last they came to Joe's.

Dave climbed
into the chair.

"Hello," said
Joe the Barber.

"H-hello,"
said Dave.

"You don't *look* all that EVIL," Dave thought out loud.

"Pardon?" said Joe the Barber, smiling.

"Oh . . . er . . . nothing!" said Dave.

Joe the Barber looked at Dave's hair.

"Can you fix it?" asked Dave.

"Yes, I can," said Joe. . . .

And he did!

Dave jumped down from the chair.

"Well?" asked his mom. "Do you like it?"

In fact, he thought it looked very, very . . .

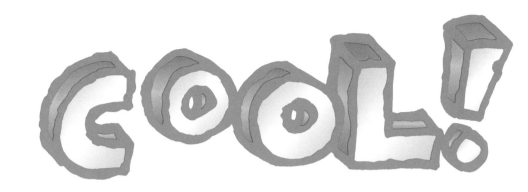

**COOL!**

It felt cool, too . . .

Hee-hee!

. . . sort of fuzzy and soft and prickly—all at the same time!

Dave didn't wear a bag on his head on the way home.

And the next day, at school . . .

teased him about his haircut—not even
Micky Badazz.

He just stared instead.

Zorro, the bunny, jumped into Dave's lap . . .

and Lunchlady Lily gave him an extra
hot dog and told him to look her up
in fifteen years.

Everyone rubbed Dave's head. . . .

# Some people even rubbed it
## TWICE!

And the NEXT
day at school . . .